Next Year I'll Be Special

Nex

Year I'll Be Special

by PATRICIA REILLY GIFF

pictures by MARYLIN HAFNER

E. P. DUTTON • NEW YORK

Library of Congress Cataloging in Publication Data

Giff, Patricia Reilly. Next year I'll be special.
SUMMARY: Marilyn describes how much different life will be next year when she is in the second grade.
[1. School stories] I. Hafner, Marylin. II. Title.
PZ7.G3626Ne [E] 79-19174 ISBN: 0-525-35810-2

Published in the United States by E. P. Dutton, a Division of Elsevier-Dutton Publishing Company, Inc., New York

Published simultaneously in Canada by Clarke, Irwin & Company Limited, Toronto and Vancouver

Editor: Ann Durell Designer: Claire Counihan

Printed in the U.S.A. First Edition
10 9 8 7 6 5 4 3 2 1

for Alice
because she's special
and
for teachers
who make children feel special

P.R.G.

for Abby, Jennifer & Amanda

M.H.

Next year, when I'm in second grade,
I won't have mean Miss Minch anymore.
Everything will be different.
Miss Lark will be my teacher.
She has long blonde hair and crinkly eyes,
and Wendy says she never yells.

As soon as
Miss Lark sees me,
she'll know I'm special.
"Marilyn," she'll say,
"would you like to be
the board washer,
or the door monitor,
or my desk duster,
or the messenger?"

"Yes," I'll say,
"I'll be all of them."

When it's time for reading,
Miss Lark will say,
"Marilyn, why are you reading
with the bottom group?

Anyone can see
you're the best reader in the class
when someone helps you
with the hard words."

In math, no one will notice
when I count on my fingers,
except Miss Lark,
and she'll just wink at me.
I won't have to rush.
I'll get all the answers right.

And Gina will say to Richard,
"Did you notice
how smart Marilyn is this year?"

When we line up for recess, Christine will say, "I want to stand next to Marilyn."

Linda will frown. "No," she'll say. "It's my turn."

"Don't fight over me, girls," I'll say.

"Christine can stand in front of me and Linda can stand in back of me."

But Karen will say, "What about me? I want to stand next to Marilyn too."

Outside, Helen will say,
"Marilyn, why are you taking
the end of the jump rope?
We want you to be first jumper."

Connie will say,
"Marilyn never misses.
She's the best jumper in the class."

All the girls and half the boys
will want to share their snacks with me.
Mary Kate will hand me her candy bar.
"Oh, Marilyn," she'll say.
"Not such a little bite.
Take a big one."

And Eric will give me his orange,
the juicy kind I love.

Even Mark will want to share
his hard-boiled egg.

"No, thank you very much," I'll say.
(I HATE eggs.)

In art I will draw a beautiful picture,
all yellow and green.

Mrs. Caro, the art teacher, will say,
"That picture is lovely.
I'm going to hang it in the hall.
All the visitors will see it."

Susan will tell Billy,
"Marilyn has fourteen pictures
hanging in the hall now."

The music teacher will ask me
to come to the piano.
"Will you sing for us, Marilyn?"
he'll ask.
Then I'll sing a song
in my A-plus voice.
"Are you going to be an opera singer
when you grow up?" the teacher will ask.
"No," I'll say,
"I'm going to be a movie star."

MUSETTAS WALTZ

There are twenty-four children
in my class, not counting me.

On Valentine's Day,
I'll get twenty-four cards
in the Valentine Box.
Everyone will want to be my valentine.

When we pack our books to go home
in the afternoon, I'll tell Miss Lark,
"You forgot to give us homework.
Miss Minch always gave us a hundred pages."

"Oh dear," Miss Lark will say. "Read some of your library book. I hope you enjoy it."

"I'll be invited
to so many birthday parties
that my mother will say,
"Marilyn, I've bought
twenty-four birthday presents
this year. You must be
the most popular girl in the class."
"What can I do?" I'll smile.
"Everyone wants me."

Daddy will say,
"Marilyn, you look different this year."

"I am different, Daddy," I'll say.
"This year I'm special."

"Oh, Marilyn," he'll say with a smile.
"You were always special to me."

Next year,
mean Miss Minch will still be in first grade.

I'll be in second with Miss Lark.
And everything will be different.

PATRICIA REILLY GIFF says, "As a reading teacher, so often I see children who are unhappy about themselves. And it seems to me that the way the teacher feels about the child spills over onto the child and to all the other children in the class. I wrote this book not only for children who are unhappy, and who wish things were different, but also for teachers....I hope that everyone who reads it will try to make other people feel special."

MARYLIN HAFNER felt that "this particular story captured, with a great deal of humor, the very common fantasy of a child's view of him/her self in relation to teachers and peers in school." She has illustrated many books for children.

The display type is set in Eastern Souvenir, Bold and Medium. The text type is Plantin #2. The line art was drawn with pencil. The book was printed at Rae Publishing Co., Inc.